DREAM
STREET

DREAM
STREET

written by
Tricia Elam Walker

collages by
Ekua Holmes
Caldecott Honoree
Coretta Scott King Medalist

a·s·b
anne schwartz books

Welcome to Dream Street—the best street in the world!
Just ask the people who live here. The houses and the dreams inside
are different as thumbprints. The sidewalks are wide enough for
huge chalk drawings and giant hopscotch boards. Children from
all over the neighborhood come to play until the streetlights go on.

Yusef waits for his brother Biko at the corner of Humboldt Avenue and Dream Street. He's thinking about how their mom always says, "Don't leave the house without your crown." She likes to tell them stories about their ancestors, who were queens and kings with dreams they never gave up on.

Each morning, unless it's raining, Mr. Sidney reads the newspaper on his stoop, dressed "to the nines," Ms. Sarah likes to say. "What's the nines?" a child will ask, and Ms. Sarah will answer, "Fancy, fancy!" Mr. Sidney is a retired mail carrier living his dream of never having to wear a uniform again. He tips his big brown fedora and greets everyone with, "Don't wait to *have* a great day. *Create* one!"

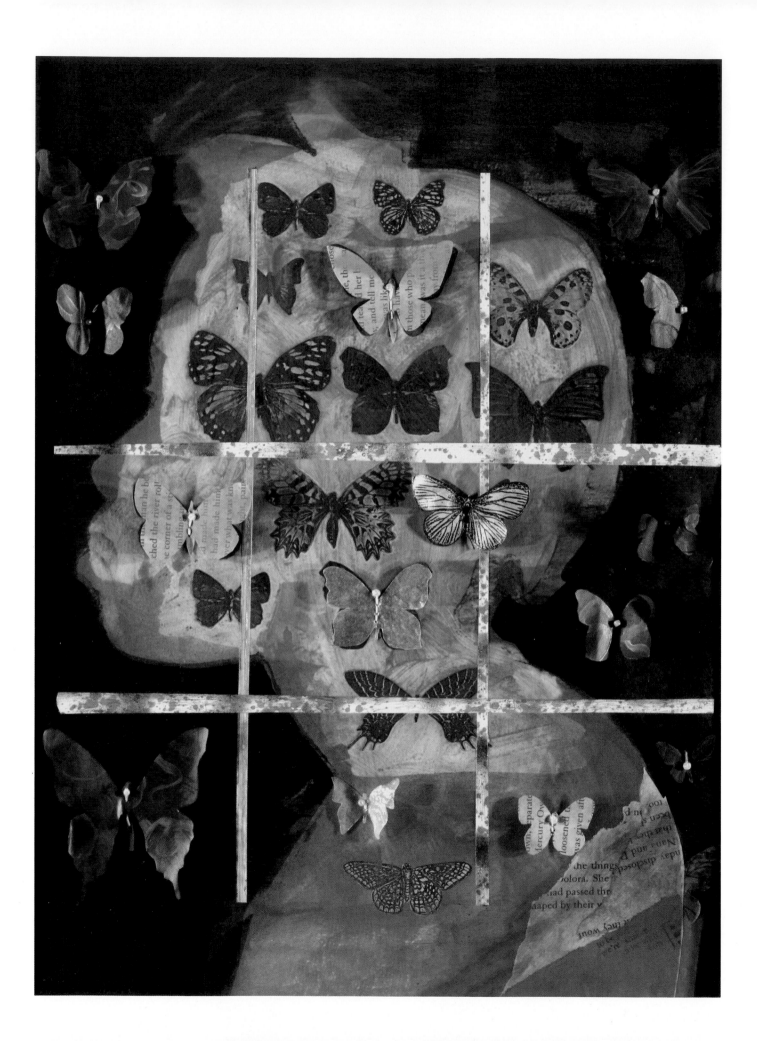

Belle catches butterflies in a jar when they fly near Ms. Sarah's birdbath, but she always lets them go before too long. "Everything has a right to be free," she says. "And every butterfly is different. Just like snowflakes and people and dreams." Belle wants to become a scientist who studies butterflies. She says there's a special name for it: a lepidopterist.

Azaria's house is next to the park. That girl can really jump some rope! She can do Double Dutch on one leg at a time. She can turn around and touch the ground. She can jump by herself with two ropes. She can even dance, jump, and dream of winning a shiny trophy one day, all at the same time. When she flies down the street, swinging her rope, she lifts her long brown legs as high as the sun.

Ms. Sarah, also known as the Hat Lady, is Belle's great-auntie. Her voice is only a whisper, but there are stories between the lines of her face that she'll share when you come close. She has lived on Dream Street longer than anyone, even longer than some of the trees, watching children turn into grown-ups and listening to their dreams along the way.

Zion walks around the corner to the library to read skyscraper-tall piles of books that take him on adventures around the world. When other kids talk or laugh, he tells them "Shhh!" because doesn't everyone know you are supposed to be quiet in there? Some days, Ms. Barbara, the librarian, hands him a brand-new book and says softly, "I have a feeling this is your cup of tea."

"Can boys be librarians?" Zion whispers to her, because it's his dream to become one.

"Of course they can!" she whispers back. He flashes a bright smile and continues his journey through the pages of the next book.

Ede lives at the top of the hill and searches for treasures that others throw away. She collects smooth rocks, broken jewelry, leaves and feathers, and adds them to her drawings of people on Dream Street. Meanwhile, her cousin, Tari, pays attention when new folks come around so she can make up stories about them. In her notebook she scribbles down the things she hears when they don't know she's listening. The cousins dream that someday they'll create a picture book together about everyone they know and meet on Dream Street.

The Phillips family has five boys—Dudley, Donald, Denardo, Dexter, and Duke, all named after jazz musicians. "Those boys are more than a handful," some say, but the brothers know not to act up or show out. On Sundays before church, their daddy, Mr. Phillips, lines them up on the front porch for inspection, from hats down to shined shoes. He dreams of forming his own jazz band with the Phillips boys one day. (Uh-oh, looks like little Duke forgot his bow tie!)

The garden behind Dessa Rae's house overflows with plants you don't see every day: purple lilies, red desert peas, and yellow passionflowers. Her magnolia trees smell like milk and honey and make your eyes feel heavy, as if they want to close. Dessa Rae's locks are so long she can wrap them around her shoulders like a shawl. Sometimes she and her grandbaby, Little Song, fall asleep together. Little Song makes sweet sounds and dreams little girl dreams.

When she was small, Ms. Paula loved to twirl on her tiptoes up and down Dream Street. Now she teaches African dance at the rec center, her head wrapped round and round with bright fabric until it's high as a pyramid. Her feet move lightning fast, slap, slap, slapping and tap, tap, tapping the floor, keeping pace with the drummer's hands. Watch out! You might get dizzy if you stare too long. Sometimes when the rhythm takes hold, her wrap unravels and falls to the ground. She never stops moving, even as she stoops down to pick it up.

Little Benjamin, who lives in the purple house next to the park, is tucked snugly into bed, but he doesn't want to go to sleep and dream. He might miss something important. He hugs his teddy bear, Tyler, who isn't ready for sleep either. Instead, they count the stars that sparkle through the bedroom window and listen to laughter outside from the big kids who don't have to go to bed yet.

The children who live and play on Dream Street can become whatever and whoever they want, because their dreams are nourished and cared for, just like Dessa Rae's flowers. There is no need to worry or to rush. They take their time, growing and playing, learning and living, and soaring skyward toward all the adventures that await them.

AUTHOR AND ILLUSTRATOR'S NOTE

The cousins Ede and Tari in this book are us, Ekua and Tricia. The story is based on our real lives and dreams growing up as a visual artist and a writer. As children, we loved what we loved (drawing and writing) and were always encouraged by friends and family. Now we know, and want you to know, that dreams do come true (with lots of hard work along the way)!

THE PHILLIPS BROTHERS' NAMESAKES

Dudley Brooks (1913–1989)—jazz pianist and composer

Donald Byrd (1932–2013)—jazz and blues trumpeter

Denardo Coleman (1956–)—jazz drummer

Dexter Gordon (1923–1990)—jazz saxophonist

Duke Ellington (1899–1974)—leader of jazz orchestra, composer

THIS BOOK IS DEDICATED TO OUR MOTHERS.

To Florence Palmerly Holmes:

Although you were small in stature, you were a strong, forthright mountain of a woman and you steadfastly displayed your love and your pride. Your regal legacy lives on through your grandson, your great-granddaughter, and your daughter, of course. I know you are proud of our work together.

To Barbara Clark Elam:

Along with all your life lessons, you taught me to love and respect words, and thus, I do. You taught me to appreciate even the smallest of moments, and I do that as well. I am a writer because you showed me the power books hold. Your love for family had no bounds, and for that, I am finally grateful. I know you are beaming over this work your niece and I created.

—T.E.W.

To Barbara Clark Elam:

A very special woman who led countless lives into the worlds of literature. Our very own librarian, storyteller, aunt, mother, counselor, encourager, and friend. I hope that this is a book you might have recommended we read together as children. A book that will make you feel proud of us.

To Florence Palmerly Holmes:

A very special woman who allowed me to dream of being an artist. A woman who taught me to keep my head to the sky and my feet on the ground. Mom, your quiet determination to give me a better life opened many doors for me. I hope this book will make you smile and know that you are the best mother I could have had.

—E.H.

Visit us on the Web! rhcbooks.com
Educators and librarians, for a variety of teaching tools, visit us at RHTeachersLibrarians.com

Library of Congress Cataloging-in-Publication Data
Names: Walker, Tricia Elam, author. | Holmes, Ekua, illustrator.
Title: Dream street / by Tricia Elam Walker ; illustrated by Ekua Holmes.
Description: First edition. | New York : Anne Schwartz Books, 2021. | Audience: Ages 4–8. | Audience: Grades K–1.
Summary: "Real-life cousins pay gorgeous homage to the street they grew up on and the loving community
that made their childhood special" —Provided by publisher.
Identifiers: LCCN 2020046360 | ISBN 978-0-525-58110-9 (hardcover)
ISBN 978-0-525-58111-6 (lib. bdg.) | ISBN 978-0-525-58112-3 (ebook)
Subjects: CYAC: Neighborhoods—Fiction. | African Americans—Fiction.
Classification: LCC PZ7.1.W3488 Dre 2021 | DDC [Fic]—dc23

The text of this book is set in 15.25-point Brandon Grotesque.
The collages were made with found and created papers, fabric, and acrylic paint.
Book design by Rachael Cole

MANUFACTURED IN CHINA
10 9 8 7 6 5 4 3 2 1
First Edition